Class No. ..........

For Megan
S.W.

ORCHARD BOOKS
338 Euston Road, London NW1 3BH
Orchard Books Australia
*Hachette Children's Books*
Level 17/207, Kent Street, Sydney, NSW 2000

ISBN 978 1 84362 529 2 (hardback)
ISBN 978 1 84362 537 7 (paperback)
First published in Great Britain in 2006
First paperback publication in 2006

1 3 5 7 9 10 8 6 4 2 (hardback)
3 5 7 9 10 8 6 4 2 (paperback)
Printed in Great Britain

# Tony Bradman

# Happy Ever After

# THE FAIRY GODMOTHER
## TAKES A BREAK

### Illustrated by Sarah Warburton

ORCHARD BOOKS

Deep in the forest there stands a little cottage, and in that cottage is a cosy bedroom, where somebody's alarm clock is about to go off...

BEEP-BEEP-BEEP! BEEP-BEEP-BEEP! BEEP-BEEP-BEEP!

"Oh no!" groaned the Fairy
Godmother. "It can't possibly be time
to get up already. I feel like I've only
just gone to bed."

5

"Sorry, dear," said her husband,
Mr Fairy Godmother. "I, er... set the
alarm for a bit earlier than usual.
I think it could be a very busy day."

"Huh, so what's new?" muttered the Fairy Godmother. She pulled the duvet over her head. "Busy, busy, busy. I never get a second to myself..."

"Oh well, never mind," said Mr FG. "I'll go and put the kettle on."

The Fairy Godmother kept muttering under the duvet.

She muttered in the shower, too, and while she got dressed, and she was still muttering when she sat down at the kitchen table. Mr FG put a nice cup of tea in front of her.

"Nobody ever thanks me, either," she said.

"Take Cinderella, for instance. I spent a whole week running around for her, putting spells on rats and mice and pumpkins and sorting out her life. And have I heard from her since?"

"Well, dear," said Mr FG, "that's probably because..."

"I'm tired of granting wishes," the Fairy Godmother muttered, interrupting him. "Anyway, where will I be waving my wand today?"

"I'll find out," said Mr FG. "I just need to switch on the computer."

Soon Mr FG was sitting before a large, glowing screen. He worked as his wife's personal assistant, and he had a special, magic computer that only accepted one kind of message - wish-mails.

RECEIVING MESSAGES...

Whenever someone in the forest made a wish, it instantly arrived on the screen with a...PING!

Mr FG tapped the keyboard, and the wish-mails started to come in. PING! PING! PING! PING! PING! PING! PING! PING! PING!...

There were far more than usual, and the screen quickly filled up.

"Right, that's it," said the Fairy
Godmother. "I've had enough.
I quit. I resign."

"And just to make it absolutely
official..."

She held up her magic wand...and
snapped it in half. Mr FG winced.

"Oh well," said Mr FG. "Er...would you like another cup of tea, dear?"

"No thanks," said the Fairy Godmother. "I'd rather have...a holiday!"

Mr FG sighed again...but he called Fairy Tale Holidays and arranged everything.

The next morning they flew out of Forest Airport, and a few hours later they arrived at Club Enchantment, their holiday destination.

"Ah, this is the life," said the Fairy Godmother as Mr FG unpacked their suitcases. "Sun, sea and sand - I can feel myself relaxing already..."

Mr and Mrs FG spent the day swimming and sunbathing (always remembering to put on sun cream) and reading their books.

In the evening they had dinner at
The Magic Spoon, Club Enchantment's
best restaurant.

The band was really cool, and the
food was a thousand times better than
Mr FG's cooking.

But the Fairy Godmother didn't seem too happy.

"Those dwarves over there are staring at me," she whispered.

"Oh no, I don't think they are, dear,"
murmured Mr FG, who was tucking into
his dinner. "This lobster is terrific. You
really should try some."

"They *are* staring at me, and I don't like it," the Fairy Godmother said. "And I'm NOT going to put up with it, either. Come on, we're leaving!"

"B-b-but..." Mr FG spluttered. Then he sighed, paid the bill, and followed his wife, looking longingly at the lovely lobster he was leaving behind.

The next morning they went to the beach again. Mr FG had just got to a good part of his book when the Fairy Godmother poked him in the ribs.

"Psst!" she hissed at him. "Somebody else is staring at me now."

"Calm down, dear," said Mr FG, looking up. "I don't think anyone... Actually, you're right. He is staring at you, isn't he? How strange."

A young troll in swimming trunks couldn't take his eyes off the Fairy Godmother.

And as they watched him, he smiled shyly, and waved. Then he said something to a family of elves nearby, and pointed at her. Soon they were smiling at her too and so was everyone else on the beach.

"You realise what this means, don't you?" the Fairy Godmother hissed to Mr FG from the corner of her mouth. *"They all know who I am!"*

"Oh, of course!" said Mr FG. "But that's no surprise. You've helped so many people, dear. There are bound to be some here who recognise you."

"They'll be asking me to grant wishes, next," she said. "And you know I won't get a word of thanks. Come on, we're leaving!"

"Yes, dear," murmured Mr FG, closing his book with a deep sigh.

That evening they didn't go to
The Magic Spoon, but to another
restaurant instead. It wasn't as good.

The Fairy Godmother wore dark
glasses and a headscarf, and didn't take
them off even when she was eating.
But people still stared at her, and smiled
and waved.

Then, the next day on the beach, the Fairy Godmother suddenly froze.

"Oh no," she whispered to Mr FG, panic in her voice. "Don't look now, but I think that princess is coming over to talk to me. Come on, we're..."

"I know, I know," muttered Mr FG. "We're leaving."

The Fairy Godmother strode off, and Mr FG hurried behind her carrying their bags, with the princess in hot pursuit.

In the end, the Fairy Godmother and Mr FG were practically running, but the princess caught up with them.

"Please, wait!" she called out. "I'm sorry, but I simply had to make sure it was you. I would never, ever forgive myself if I missed this chance to..."

"Sorry! Can't stop!" said the Fairy Godmother. "Come along, dear!"

"...say a huge thank you for everything you did for me," said the princess.

"Er...I'm Cinderella, in case you'd forgotten. You totally changed my life."

"Did I really?" said the Fairy Godmother, peering at the princess for a second, then smiling. "Yes, I remember you now. Well, how are things?"

Cinderella told the Fairy Godmother all about her new life with Prince Charming. Cinders also said she would have thanked her before, but didn't have any way of getting in touch with her.

As they talked, lots more people came up to the Fairy Godmother and said exactly the same thing.

"Anyway, enjoy the rest of your holiday," said Cinders at last. The Fairy Godmother beamed at her.

"Although I bet you can't wait to go home and start helping people again. How wonderful to have a job like yours... Bye!"

The Fairy Godmother's smile
vanished, and suddenly she looked upset.
And by the time she and Mr FG were
back in their room, she was in tears.

"Cinderella is right," she moaned. "It is a wonderful job, and I've thrown it away. Why didn't you tell me no one knows how to send me any thanks?"

"Er...I did try," said Mr FG. "Anyway, I'm sure that's a problem I can solve. You need to get out a bit more too, maybe do some follow-up visits."

"Follow-ups to what?" she wailed.
"I won't be able to grant wishes any
more. I broke my wand, remember?
Although now I *so* wish that I hadn't..."

"Well...your wish is granted," said
Mr FG, smiling. He opened one of their
suitcases and pulled out...her wand.
"Sort of, anyway. I mended it before we
left home. And though I say so myself,
it's, er...almost as good as new."

The Fairy Godmother looked at it in
amazement...and hugged him.

They enjoyed the rest of their holiday.
And even though there were loads
of wish-mails waiting for them when
they got home, the Fairy Godmother
didn't mind.

In fact, she was keen to get back to work now that she felt more appreciated. Mr FG rather liked having the cottage to himself too...

So the Fairy Godmother and Mr FG and just about everyone in the forest who made a wish lived...

HAPPILY EVER AFTER!